THE WINDMILL'S SECRET

A Darkspire Chronicles Adventure
Book One

JPS Nagi

For more information, or to book an event, contact :
Author@JPSNagi.com
http://www.PlanetNagi.com

Book design by JPS Nagi
Cover design by JPS Nagi

ISBN – Paperback: 978-1-966767-05-3
ISBN – eBook: 978-1-966767-06-0

First Edition: January 2026
Library of Congress Control Number: 2025923912

To my parents –
who, without being readers themselves, filled my childhood with books.

You surrounded me with stories long before I could understand their worth, and in doing so, gave me the greatest gift: a love of words, of imagination, and of worlds beyond my own.

This story, like so many others in my life, is rooted in the quiet seeds you planted.

AUTHOR'S NOTE

Stories often begin not with answers, but with questions. What lies beneath the surface of a quiet town? What secrets do old walls keep when no one is listening? Why do the shadows sometimes linger longer than they should?

The **Darkspire Chronicles** was born out of these questions. It is not one tale, but many: a shared universe of standalone adventures bound together by mystery, shadow, and the timeless call to step beyond the familiar into the unknown. Each Chronicle tells the story of a different place, a different secret, a different threshold crossed – but all of them share the same heartbeat: the sense that even in ordinary places, something extraordinary waits to be uncovered.

At the heart of these stories are unlikely companions – wanderers, rogues, hunters, healers, seekers – drawn together by circumstance, by duty, or by fate. Their journeys are rarely grand at the start. They begin with whispers in taverns, strange happenings at the edges of villages, or a relic stirring after centuries of silence. And yet, these small beginnings ripple outward into moments that test courage, loyalty, and the very core of who these adventurers are.

In that way, the Darkspire Chronicles is not just a collection of fantasy stories. It is an ongoing exploration of what it means to confront the unknown: the secrets hidden in the world, and the shadows that live within ourselves.

Book One: *The Windmill's Secret*

Every Chronicle must begin somewhere. For this one, it begins in a small farming village called Eldermire.

At first glance, Eldermire is ordinary – cobbled streets, the smell of bread from the ovens, orchards buzzing with bees, children's laughter on the green. But at the crest of the hill stands the windmill, and here the ordinary ends. Its sails groan and turn **against the wind**, as though bound to a rhythm no breeze commands. For the villagers, it is a source of unease, something spoken of in whispers. For the adventurers passing through – Kaelen, Mira, Tav, and Serneya – it is the beginning of a mystery that will pull them into the depths of something far older than the village itself.

The Windmill's Secret is the first tale in the **Darkspire Chronicles**. It is a story of small beginnings that lead to dangerous depths, of ordinary lives entangled with ancient relics, of companions tested not only by shadows in the world but by the desires and doubts within their own hearts.

As you read, you step with them into Eldermire, into the whispering shadows beneath the mill, into the secret that refuses to stay hidden. And if you listen closely, you may hear it – the quiet turning of unseen gears, the grinding of forces older than stone, the truth that waits in the dark.

This is where the Chronicles begin. But the road beyond Eldermire stretches far, and many more shadows remain to be told.

JPS Nagi
September 9, 2025
Portland, Oregon

ACKNOWLEDGEMENTS

First, I want to thank **Tony**, who was the first to act on my endless questions about role-playing games. He created my very first character, set up a session, and gave me a glimpse of what awaited beyond the dice. He also had to roll back that character's strength once he realized he'd accidentally made me a walking fortress – a "tank" who could bulldoze half his carefully designed encounters. That first session was chaos, laughter, and imagination in its purest form and it hooked me for life.

To everyone who sat around our RPG table – **Robert**, **Chris**, **Michael**, **Audryana**, and my daughter **Khushi** – thank you. You brought life to every moment and turned stories into shared adventures. The memories we built together – both the triumphs and the disasters – became the foundation for the worlds I now write.

To **Dhruv** and **Pankaj**, my friends and brothers, who have always supported me quietly but unwaveringly, thank you for your faith and patience – even when I disappear into imaginary worlds for days at a time.

To **Alfonso**, my *ink-and-pen brother* in both life and story – thank you for constantly urging me to write more, for reading my drafts, challenging my ideas, and reminding me that storytelling, like art, is a craft best shared.

And finally, to **Gitanjali**, who has listened to more of my half-told tales than anyone should have to and who often fell asleep halfway through them – thank you. Your quiet presence and belief in me are what let me keep dreaming, even when the words come slowly.

This book, like all stories worth telling, is the sum of many voices. I'm grateful to all of you for lending me yours.

CONTENTS

P

The windmill had always been loyal.

Roric Branthorne knew its voice better than his own heartbeat – the creak of timber that had stood against three generations of storms, the patient groan of gears that turned grain into bread, the steady sigh of sails catching the hilltop wind. It had been his charge since youth, a trust passed down from his father, and his father's father before him. The mill's rhythms were the rhythms of Eldermire itself.

But tonight, those rhythms were wrong.

Roric stood in the dim glow of a single lantern, its light a trembling circle against the stone walls of his cottage. The sound came not from the sails above – there was no wind tonight, not even a breath to stir the grass – but from below. A grinding, slow and ponderous, like iron teeth chewing stone.

He rubbed his calloused hands together, trying to chase the cold that had settled into his bones. "Not possible," he muttered. "Can't be." The words tasted brittle in the air, a defense against the truth he already feared.

At first, he had ignored it. A keeper's mind, he told himself, too long alone, inventing noises where there were none. But the grinding came again the next night. And the night after. Soon it was joined by drafts – cold fingers snaking up from the floor, carrying the metallic tang of rust and something sharper, something he could not name.

And then the shadows came.

Roric had been mending sacks in the loft when he saw them: not the kind cast by lantern or moon, but shapes that slid against the walls with no source, lengthening and recoiling like smoke caught in reverse. They pooled near the grain hatch, then slithered downward, vanishing between the cracks of the boards. His lantern flame guttered, though the air was still.

That night, he bolted the hatch.

But bolts did not silence the gears.

Now, weeks later, he could bear it no longer. He had waited for the mayor to ask, for the villagers to speak plainly of their fears, but no one dared. Eldermire had learned the same lesson as he: some things were better left undisturbed. And yet, the sails of the mill had begun to turn against the wind, and every farmer, every shepherd, every child who looked up at the hill could see it.

Roric set the lantern on the floor and shoved aside the sacks of grain with a grunt. The boards beneath were worn smooth where generations of Branthornes had trod, but one square bore the dark iron latch of the hatch. He stared at it a long moment, lips pressed thin.

"You've run well for me," he whispered to the mill above, as though the structure itself might hear. "Don't turn against me now."

He crouched, fitted the key into the lock, and turned. The bolt gave with a heavy clunk. The hatch groaned as he pulled it open.

Air rushed up – cold, damp, and old. The lantern flame dipped low, nearly extinguished. Roric swallowed, lifted the lantern, and began to descend.

The stairs spiraled downward into blackness. Each step echoed too loudly, as though the stone itself resented the sound. The grinding grew louder, layered now with a faint hum, deep and low, like the vibration of a string drawn tight across the world. His breath frosted in the air.

The chamber at the bottom was larger than he remembered from his boyhood – a vault of stone and shadow. Massive iron cogs jutted from floor and ceiling, turning without wind, without water, without reason. Their teeth bit into one another with inexorable patience, grinding, grinding. The sound seemed to thrum inside his skull.

At the center stood the pedestal.

It was simple granite, waist-high, carved by hands long dead. Roric's father had shown it to him once, years ago, when he was barely old enough to climb the stairs. "A relic," he'd said. "Old as the mill itself. Don't touch it. Don't speak of it. Just remember it's here."

Roric remembered. And he had obeyed. Until tonight.

The pedestal was no longer empty.

Something rested in the shallow depression: a sphere of black crystal, veined with faint crimson. The veins pulsed faintly, like embers under ash, steady and alive. The lantern light seemed to bend away from it, as though the orb swallowed more than shadow – it swallowed certainty.

Roric froze. His mind told him to run, to slam the hatch shut and bar it forever. But his feet carried him forward.

The closer he drew, the colder the air became. His breath plumed in clouds. The hum deepened, not in volume but in intimacy, as if it had crawled inside his chest and found his ribs for a drum. His hand lifted, unbidden, to touch –

And then the shadows stirred.

They poured from the orb in slow tendrils, rising like smoke in water. They crept along the walls, over the cogs, up the stairs. They did not rush him. They surrounded him.

And then he heard it.

Not with ears, not with mind, but with something deeper: a voice that was not a voice, whispering in the hollow between his thoughts.

You are tired, Roric Branthorne. You've carried the mill alone. Let me turn the sails. Let me grind the grain. Let me shoulder what you no longer can.

His knees buckled. His hand brushed the stone of the pedestal, and cold lanced up his arm like a frozen nail. He jerked back with a hoarse cry, the lantern falling, shattering against the stone. Shadows surged at the light's death, then retreated again, patient, waiting.

Roric scrambled for the stairs, heart hammering, breath ragged. The voice followed him all the way up.

You cannot bar the wind. You cannot bar me. I am already turning.

He slammed the hatch shut, bolted it, and staggered back. His cottage seemed suddenly too small, its walls too thin. Above, the sails of the mill groaned once, then turned – slowly, deliberately – against the still night air.

Roric pressed his back to the wall, staring up at the ceiling. His hands shook. His breath came ragged.

He knew then, with a certainty that hollowed him: the mill was no longer his.

And Eldermire, for all its orchards and fields and laughter, was already in the grip of something older than stone and darker than shadow.

1

A WIND THAT BLOWS THE WRONG WAY

The road to Eldermire stretched like a ribbon of pale earth across the springtime hills, winding between patches of wildflowers and fields freshly tilled for planting. The air was sweet with the fragrance of apple orchards and damp soil, the kind of smell that promised new growth, long days, and warm evenings spent beneath the stars. For a time, the four travelers said nothing. They let the rhythm of hoofbeats and the occasional call of a lark set the pace, content to breathe in the season's promise.

Kaelen Thorne, riding slightly ahead, broke the silence first. The half-elf sat straight in his saddle, his lean frame balanced with the natural ease of one who had spent more of his life on the move than at rest. His hawk, Bristle, circled lazily above, dipping a wing to catch the thermals rising from the valley. Kaelen's amber eyes, sharp and steady, were not on the road but on the horizon. He pulled his horse to a halt, lifting a gloved hand to shade his gaze.

"Strange," he murmured.

Behind him, Mira Valeheart guided her mare forward until she was level with him. She was human, with sun-touched hair that glowed like copper in the light, and a pendant of Lathander hanging over the front of her travel-stained robes. She followed Kaelen's line of sight and frowned. "What is it?"

Kaelen pointed. "The wind's from the east."

She tilted her head, puzzled. "And?"

He nodded toward the far hill where Eldermire nestled in the valley. Beyond the slate roofs and cobblestone lanes, on its own gentle rise, stood the windmill – old, proud, and stubborn. Its sails turned slow and steady, but their motion was unmistakably wrong. They spun west, straining against the invisible hand of the east wind.

Mira's brow furrowed. "That shouldn't be possible." She crossed herself instinctively, tracing the sunburst over her chest. "Unless..." Her words faded, but the implication hung in the air – unless some power other than the wind was driving it.

A snort came from behind them. Tavric Underbough, who had been humming some jaunty tune while perched atop his stout little pony, leaned to the side for a better view. His patched cloak – half a dozen different fabrics stitched together in colors that clashed and yet somehow suited him – flared out behind him as he grinned.

"Or maybe," he said, "it's just broken." He scratched at his beard, the smirk widening. "You know how villages are. They've probably been patching that thing with spit and prayer for fifty years. Maybe the sails just don't know which way they're supposed to spin anymore."

Kaelen gave him a flat look. "You don't believe that."

Tav winked. "Of course not. But it's comforting to pretend."

At the rear rode Serneya Duskbane, her hood drawn low so that her horns curved like black crescents beneath its edge. The tiefling's eyes glowed faintly in the shade, golden pools that reflected more than they revealed. She had been silent since they left the crossroads that morning, but now her gaze fixed on the windmill, unblinking.

"It isn't broken," she said at last, her voice low, as if speaking too loudly might draw something's attention. "It's moving with purpose. Something beneath it is calling."

No one replied immediately. The sails creaked faintly even at this distance, and the sound carried down the wind like the groan of some ancient beast.

Mira shifted uneasily in her saddle. "Eldermire is supposed to be peaceful. A farming village, nothing more."

"They usually are," Kaelen replied. He loosened the strap of his quiver, scanning the road ahead.

Tav clucked to his pony, nudging it forward with a whistle. "Well, haunted windmills or not, the inn will have cider, and I don't know about you lot, but I plan to sample it before deciding if this place is cursed. Priorities."

The others followed, though their thoughts were heavier than his words suggested.

The road descended into the valley, the first signs of the village emerging around them. Orchards lined the slopes, their branches white with blossoms. Bees hummed lazily from bloom to bloom, oblivious to the unease shadowing the land. Stone walls bordered fields of young barley and rye, and the path itself grew smoother, worn by countless wagon wheels bringing produce to market.

Eldermire revealed itself slowly: cottages with slate roofs and ivy creeping up their walls, gardens full of herbs and vegetables, children darting across lanes with shrill laughter. A smith's hammer rang in rhythm from somewhere within, and the faint smell of baking bread wafted on the air. To a casual eye, it was the picture of pastoral calm.

Yet as they passed, Kaelen noticed the way some villagers' glances lingered on the travelers. Eyes darted toward the hill where the windmill turned, then back to the strangers, as if measuring whether they might be the sort who meddled – or solved problems.

Mira gave a small, reassuring smile to a woman who clutched her child's hand tightly as they crossed the street. The woman nodded, but her gaze quickly flicked upward, back to the sails above.

The closer they drew, the louder the creaking became. It was not the steady groan of wood and gear, but a grinding note out of harmony with the wind. Like a heartbeat, Kaelen thought grimly, but one that pulsed against the world instead of with it.

At the crest of the lane, they reined in once more. The windmill stood tall above them, its weathered stones streaked with lichen, its sails straining like the limbs of a thing alive. The sky was clear, the breeze steady, and yet its rhythm fought against both.

Tav let out a low whistle. "Well, there's our welcome sign. Makes you wonder if the ale here flows backward, too."

"Don't joke," Mira said softly. She adjusted her pendant, her knuckles whitening around the chain.

Serneya's gaze lingered, unflinching. "It doesn't matter whether it's curse or machine. Something lies beneath that hill. And it's waiting for us."

For a moment, none of them spoke. The village bustled quietly below, the orchard trees swayed, the smith's hammer rang. Life went on as though nothing were wrong. And yet above it all, the windmill's groan was a reminder: the world did not always spin the way it should.

Kaelen straightened in his saddle. "Then let's see what Eldermire has to say for itself."

With that, they nudged their mounts forward, toward the

heart of the village – and toward the whispers that awaited them at the inn.

2

THE WHISPERING WILLOW

he Whispering Willow Inn sat at the center of Eldermire like a hearth at the heart of a home. Its weathered sign swayed gently from iron chains, the painted willow tree upon it faded with years but still graceful, its branches curving protectively around the words. A narrow stream ran beside the inn, murmuring over smooth stones, and the sweet smell of bread and herbs drifted from its open windows. On any other evening, the inn should have been alive with laughter, music, and the easy banter of a village untroubled.

But tonight, the mood was different.

As Kaelen pushed the door open, the warm air of the common room enveloped them. The fire in the great hearth blazed bright, throwing golden light across timber beams darkened by smoke and age. Lanterns hung in niches, and the tables were crowded with villagers – farmers in earth-stained boots, shepherds smelling faintly of wool, merchants with travel packs at their feet. The scents of spiced cider, roasted lamb, and onion soup mingled thick in the air.

Yet beneath all the warmth was a palpable hush. Conversations that should have been merry were muted, voices pitched low, and every so often a pair of eyes darted toward the door as if expecting trouble to walk through. When the strangers entered, those eyes fixed on them for a moment too long before sliding away.

Mira noticed it first – the unease, the stiffness in the shoulders of patrons who should have been relaxed after a day's labor. "They're afraid," she murmured, adjusting the pendant at her throat.

Tav gave her a cheeky grin. "Or they've just never seen a halfling this handsome." He swept his patched cloak theatrically before sauntering to the bar. The innkeeper, a stout woman with arms like kneaded dough, raised an eyebrow but said nothing as he slid onto a stool.

Kaelen moved through the room with a hunter's instinct, eyes scanning for subtle signs. A farmer hunched too close to his mug, knuckles white around the handle. Two older men leaned together in the corner, their voices hushed. A serving girl carried a tray too quickly, her eyes flicking toward the windows whenever the wind rattled the shutters.

Serneya lingered near the fire, her golden eyes catching the flames. She didn't need to hear words to sense the tension; it hummed in the air like a string pulled taut.

Tav cleared his throat, louder than necessary. "Two ciders, please," he said to the innkeeper. Then, with deliberate nonchalance, he let his ears tilt toward the corner where the old men whispered.

"...turning the wrong way again," one muttered, his voice low but sharp.

"...started after the winter's thaw... hasn't stopped since," replied the other, casting a wary glance toward the door.

Tav's grin widened. He sipped from the mug the innkeeper slid toward him and muttered into the foam, "Well, that's our topic of conversation, isn't it?"

Kaelen joined him at the bar, his tone more direct. "The windmill. What do the villagers say of it?"

The innkeeper's hands paused mid-polish on a tankard. For a heartbeat, her eyes flicked toward the hill, though the walls hid the view. "Folk say many things," she replied carefully. "That it's cursed. Haunted. That something lives beneath it. Best not to repeat such talk."

"We prefer truth to rumors," Mira said gently. Her voice carried the calm authority of a priestess, and though she smiled warmly, her eyes did not waver. "If Eldermire suffers, we would help."

The innkeeper's mouth pressed into a thin line, but she gave a small nod toward the corner table. "Roric knows more than any. The windmill's his charge."

Kaelen followed her gaze. The name had surfaced often enough in whispers: Roric, the keeper of the mill. A recluse, they had heard, and not inclined to share his troubles with outsiders.

The serving girl, emboldened by Serneya's steady gaze, set down her tray and leaned closer. Her voice was barely above a whisper. "It isn't just the sails. Folk say they've seen shadows at its base. Moving when no lantern's lit." She shivered, then hurried away, cheeks flushed.

Mira exchanged a glance with Kaelen, her unease plain. Shadows where there should be none was seldom a good sign.

Tav drained the last of his cider with a flourish. "Well then," he said brightly, "looks like we'll be paying Mister Roric a visit."

"Not so fast," Kaelen said, his tone even. "If the whole village whispers but no one acts, there's reason. He won't welcome us."

Serneya's eyes glinted in the firelight. "He doesn't need to welcome us. We only need him to talk."

The fire crackled. Outside, the wind rattled the shutters again, and for an instant the sails of the mill creaked, their unnatural rhythm carrying faintly even here. Every conversation in the inn faltered. All eyes flicked toward the sound, then quickly back to their mugs.

Mira rose from her seat, her voice quiet but resolute. "If the people of Eldermire will not face this, then we must. Roric holds the key."

Kaelen gave a short nod. "At dawn, then."

But Tav was already on his feet, cloak flaring behind him as he headed for the door. "Why wait for dawn? Haunted windmills don't keep office hours."

Serneya followed without a word, the firelight fading from her golden eyes as the door swung open to the cool night air.

The others exchanged glances, then joined them. Behind, the inn resumed its muted rhythm, but the whispers were sharper now, quicker, as if the villagers could sense that something had shifted – that strangers had taken the first step toward a truth no one else dared to touch.

Above the rooftops, the sails of the windmill still turned stubbornly against the wind.

3

THE KEEPER OF THE MILL

he road up to the windmill wound steeply, bordered by wild grass and briar. From below, the sails had looked merely stubborn; up close, they loomed like the limbs of some vast creature struggling against invisible bonds. Each turn was a groan of timber and iron, a sound that echoed in the bones more than the ears. The air carried the faint tang of oil and rust, sharp beneath the sweeter scents of orchard and field.

At the hill's crest, a squat stone dwelling nestled against the windmill's base. Smoke curled lazily from its chimney, but no lamp shone in its windows. The path to the door was worn smooth, yet Kaelen noticed the absence of fresh footprints. Last night's rain should have left muddy tracks. There were none.

He signaled to the others, and they dismounted, boots crunching on the gravel. Tav strode ahead, whistling low as if to announce himself, and rapped his knuckles against the heavy oak door.

It opened after a moment, not cautiously but firmly, as though the man behind it had little patience for hesitation.

Roric stood in the threshold. He was tall but wiry, his frame lean from years of labor, his hair shot through with gray. His hands bore the ingrained stains of oil and grain dust alike, and his pale blue eyes fixed on them with the wary sharpness of a hawk sighting movement in the grass.

"I'll thank you to leave me to my work," he said without greeting. His voice was rough, a rasp that carried both weariness and iron.

Mira stepped forward, her palms open in a gesture of peace. "We mean no trouble. But the village is concerned about the mill. They say it hasn't been right for months."

"Not your concern," Roric said flatly. "Not your windmill."

Kaelen met the man's gaze without flinching. "You know as well as we do that a windmill should follow the breeze, not fight against it. Whatever's driving those sails isn't natural."

Tav leaned against the doorframe with a grin that was equal parts charm and provocation. "And let's be honest – you don't strike me as the sort of fellow who oils his lock, hides a hatch, and pretends nothing's wrong. You've been poking around down there, haven't you?"

Roric's eyes narrowed. "You've got sharp tongues for strangers."

"Better than sharp swords," Tav quipped.

The faintest twitch crossed Roric's weathered face – irritation, perhaps, or the ghost of a smile. His gaze slid past Tav to Serneya, who stood a little apart, her golden eyes unblinking.

"You've felt it, haven't you?" he asked her, surprising the others.

Serneya inclined her head slightly. "The wind doesn't move your mill. Something else does."

The words hung heavy in the air. For a moment, Roric's hand tightened on the doorframe as though he might slam it shut. But then he exhaled, long and slow, and stepped back.

"Come in," he said.

The interior of the dwelling was plain, its furnishings sparse but orderly. Tools hung neatly on pegs. A kettle hissed on the stove. Grain sacks were stacked against one wall, their burlap rough and worn. The smell of oil was stronger here, mingling with the earthy scent of flour.

Roric crossed to the hearth, where he stirred the kettle absently before speaking. "Few months back, it started turning wrong. No change in the winds, no storm to blame. One night, I heard the machinery grinding below though the sails stood still. There's a cellar under the mill, older than this house. I've avoided it as long as I could, but..." His voice dropped. "Sometimes, at night, I hear more than gears. Drafts that don't belong. Whispers. Like the stone itself is breathing."

Mira shivered. "Why didn't you tell the mayor?"

"Because Alaric Bramblewood likes neat answers and tidy ledgers," Roric snapped. "This isn't something he'd understand – or want to."

Kaelen knelt near the grain sacks and brushed his fingers across the floorboards. There – faint grooves, the marks of something heavy dragged more than once. "You've a hatch beneath these," he said.

Roric hesitated, then nodded. "Aye. Locked it years ago. But locks don't keep shadows out."

Tav crouched beside Kaelen, rapping his knuckles on the wood. "Solid, but not too clever. I could have it open before you finish your next breath."

"Leave it," Roric said quickly.

Kaelen rose, his expression firm. "You know as well as I do that whatever's beneath there isn't going away on its own."

Silence stretched. The sails groaned again outside, the sound seeping through the walls. Finally, Roric rubbed a hand over his face, weary lines deepening.

"I've kept this mill running for twenty years," he said. "I know its voice, its aches, its moods. This isn't the work of weather or wear. It's something else. And if you're fool enough to go down there, I won't stop you. But don't say I didn't warn you."

His eyes met Kaelen's, then Mira's, then Serneya's in turn. At last, he stepped aside, gesturing to the sacks. "The hatch is yours."

Kaelen gave a curt nod. Mira touched Roric's arm briefly, her voice softer. "You've carried this burden alone long enough. We'll face what waits below."

Roric didn't answer. He only turned back to the kettle, stirring it though it no longer needed stirring.

The four companions moved to the grain sacks, ready to uncover the hatch. The air seemed colder here, as though the shadows beneath the floor were already reaching upward to greet them.

4

BENEATH THE MILL

The grain sacks were heavier than they looked. Kaelen dragged the first aside, burlap scratching against his palms, and Tav made quick work of the rest with the nimble energy of someone who enjoyed prying into secrets. Beneath the pile lay a hatch of thick oak, its iron fittings black with age yet polished in places where fingers had touched it too often. Kaelen crouched, running his hand across the edges. The boards were cleaner than the rest of the floor – no dust, no flour. This hatch had been opened recently. He glanced up at Roric.

"You've been down there," he said.

The miller stood stiff, arms folded. His eyes flicked toward the hatch, then away, as though unwilling to look at it too long. "Once. That was enough."

The lock itself was sturdy but not extraordinary, a stout piece of iron fastened through the latch. Tav knelt beside it, rubbing his hands together like a priest before prayer. "Nice craftsmanship," he said cheerfully. "But not nice enough."

He slid a pair of slender picks from his belt pouch and worked them with practiced ease. The sound was faint – click, scrape, whisper – and then a soft, final snick. The lock yielded with a sigh. Tav held it up like a trophy. "And that, ladies and gentlemen, is how you open doors to doom."

The hatch groaned as Kaelen heaved it open. At once, a draft of air rushed upward, cold and stale, as though drawn from the lungs of a buried crypt. The smell of damp stone and rust mingled with something sharper – metallic, like a copper coin pressed to the tongue. Mira grimaced and instinctively touched the pendant at her chest.

The stairs spiraled downward, cut into stone that glistened faintly with moisture. The lamplight Roric handed them seemed to shrink as Kaelen descended first, each step creaking under his boots. The sound of the sails above faded with every turn, replaced by a deeper noise: a slow grinding, rhythmic and low, like the rumble of a sleeping giant.

"Do you hear that?" Mira whispered as she followed. "It sounds alive."

"It's machinery," Roric's voice drifted down from above, but it lacked conviction.

Serneya trailed last, her golden eyes reflecting the lamp's glow. She did not answer, but her head tilted slightly, listening as if to a voice beneath the grinding. Her lips moved silently, shaping words none of them recognized.

The stair ended in a broad chamber, its walls and ceiling of rough-hewn stone. Water trickled somewhere unseen, the droplets tapping in slow rhythm. Enormous iron cogs jutted from the floor and ceiling, each turning ponderously with no shaft or chain to drive them. Their teeth clashed in perfect timing, though there was no power to move them – no wind, no waterwheel, nothing.

Kaelen touched one cautiously. It was cold, far too cold for metal that had been grinding against itself for months. He pulled his hand back quickly.

In the center of the chamber stood a pedestal, carved from a single block of granite, waist-high and perfectly smooth. Its top bore a shallow depression, circular, the faint outline of something once set there. Dust coated the rest of the chamber in thick blankets, but the depression was clean – as if whatever had rested there still claimed the space.

Mira's breath caught. "It was holding something."

"Not holding," Serneya corrected, her voice low. "Binding."

Kaelen crouched near the base of the pedestal. His sharp eyes traced faint scuff marks – bootprints, no more than a day old, leading to and from the stairs. Smaller than Roric's feet. Lighter. "Someone's been here recently," he murmured. "And they took whatever was bound here."

Beside the pedestal, a folded parchment lay half-buried in dust. Its seal was cracked, stamped with the crest of Eldermire – a stylized oak leaf flanked by sheaves of wheat. Kaelen lifted it, brushing away grit, and handed it to Mira.

She broke the rest of the seal and scanned the ink. "'By order of Mayor Alaric Bramblewood...'" she read aloud, her voice tightening. "'Maintenance of the mill is to be recorded in detail. Any anomalies are to be reported at once.'" She lowered the letter, her brow furrowed. "So he knew. At least enough to issue orders."

"Or to cover his tracks," Tav said, peering into the depression atop the pedestal. "Looks like something round. Orb-shaped, maybe." He shivered. "I don't like it. Feels like staring at a seat still warm after the sitter's gone."

Mira glanced at Serneya, who had stepped closer to the pedestal. The tiefling's eyes were fixed on the hollow, her breath shallow.

"What is it?" Mira asked softly.

Serneya blinked once, slowly, before answering. "It isn't empty. The shape is gone, yes – but the shadow of it remains. You can feel it in the air, can't you? It clings."

And indeed they all felt it now, the weight of the room pressing against their skin. Not the heaviness of damp stone, but a subtle distortion, like the silence after a scream or the stillness before a storm.

The grinding of the unseen cogs grew louder, though their pace never quickened. It was as if the chamber itself was aware of their intrusion, the machinery a heartbeat in the dark.

Kaelen straightened, folding the letter and tucking it away. "Whatever was here, it's gone now. And whoever took it left through the manor."

Mira's jaw tightened. "Then the mayor has questions to answer."

From above, the sails groaned again, the sound echoing faintly through the stone walls. For a heartbeat, it seemed as if the grinding cogs were answering in kind.

5

THE MAYOR'S PROBLEM

The manor of Alaric Bramblewood dominated the heart of Eldermire, its slate roof and stone walls rising above the clustered cottages like a reminder that leadership demanded stature. Built in the old style, it was more fortress than home – arched windows set deep into thick masonry, doors of oak bound in iron, and chimneys that smoked heavily even on mild days. Though trimmed hedges and a cobbled courtyard softened its face, the building exuded weight, as though pressing its authority onto the village around it.

Two guards flanked the iron gate, their armor polished but their eyes weary. As the companions approached, one shifted his spear nervously. "You're the strangers Roric sent, then? The mayor will want words. He's not in the mood for niceties."

Kaelen gave a short nod. "Neither are we."

Inside, the manor bustled with activity. Servants carried trays, messengers hurried down halls, guards clattered across marble floors. Yet for all the movement, there was a tension threaded through it, like a loom pulled too tight. Conversations faltered as the strangers passed, and more than one servant cast a nervous glance at the companions' weapons.

The steward led them into a high-ceilinged study lined with shelves. Ledgers and tomes filled every alcove, their spines worn by decades of record-keeping. Maps of Eldermire and the surrounding farmlands hung on the walls, annotated with neat notes in a precise hand. Behind a broad desk stood Mayor Alaric Bramblewood.

He was a man built as solidly as his home: broad shoulders, thick neck, hands that had once known work before they knew ink. His silver hair was pulled back neatly, and his green velvet doublet was fastened with polished brass buttons that caught the light. His eyes – hard, sharp, and calculating – swept over the group like an appraiser evaluating a lot of livestock.

"You're outsiders," he said without preamble. His voice was deep, clipped. "And yet Roric lets you meddle in his mill." He gestured to the chairs before his desk but did not sit himself. "Very well. If you wish to stick your noses into Eldermire's affairs, then you'll hear what has befallen us."

Kaelen crossed his arms, standing instead of sitting. "We already know of the windmill. But there's more. Something was taken from beneath it." He withdrew the folded letter from his pouch and placed it on the desk. "This bears your seal."

Bramblewood's eyes narrowed as he picked it up. "So you've been snooping." His tone carried no shame – only irritation at being caught. He set the parchment aside with deliberate calm. "Yes. I gave instructions to Roric. The mill has been behaving strangely, and as mayor I must ensure it continues its purpose. That doesn't mean I know why it does what it does."

Mira stepped forward, her voice warm but firm. "Then perhaps you can explain the theft. Your household guards the relics of Eldermire, does it not?"

At that, Bramblewood's jaw tightened. He turned toward the empty display case along the far wall, its velvet-lined stand conspicuously bare. Dust still clung in the shape of what had once rested there: a long, gem-encrusted sword.

"My ceremonial blade," he said, his tone hardening. "Forged by Eldermire's first blacksmith, carried by every mayor since. A symbol of my office, and of this village's endurance." He paused, his hand clenching at his side. "It was taken last night."

"Taken how?" Tav asked, tilting his head. "Big sword, heavy hilt, all those shiny gems – not exactly the sort of thing you slip into your boot."

"The case was locked. My guards were at their posts. Yet when I entered this morning, the sword was gone." Bramblewood's lips pressed thin. "Not a scratch on the lock. Not a footprint in the dust."

Serneya's golden gaze drifted to the case. "Perhaps the thief left no footprints because they were not entirely... flesh."

Bramblewood frowned but did not dismiss the idea. "I have questioned my staff and my watch. Their answers are contradictory, their memories clouded. You will speak to them yourselves."

He clapped his hands, and within moments, a trio of nervous figures filed into the room: the manor's cook, the butler, and a young maid. Each bore the pinched expression of someone dragged unwillingly into scrutiny.

The cook spoke first, her voice trembling. "I saw... someone. A cloaked figure, passing through the kitchens after midnight. Tall, but moved quick. I thought, " she swallowed. "I thought it a dream until the sword was gone."

The butler, stiff-backed, shook his head firmly. "I saw nothing. Heard nothing. No one entered these halls under my watch." Yet his eyes flicked once toward the empty case, betraying unease.

The maid clutched her apron. "I woke in the night. There were shadows in the corridor – shadows moving when no lantern burned." She crossed herself quickly. "And then they vanished."

The companions exchanged glances. Kaelen's expression hardened. Mira's eyes filled with quiet resolve. Tav whistled low, his grin fading. Serneya's gaze lingered on the girl. "Not all shadows come from light," she murmured.

Bramblewood dismissed the servants with a sharp wave, then leaned over his desk. His eyes fixed on the adventurers. "Find my sword. Whoever stole it has already defied my guard and my household. If you cross their path, you will not be spared their cunning. But bring it back, and Eldermire will owe you more than gratitude."

He straightened, his tone heavy with finality. "Fail, and the mill will be the least of our worries."

Outside, the wind groaned against the manor's shutters. Far above the rooftops, the sails of the windmill creaked, still fighting the breeze as if mocking the mayor's command.

6

THE CHASE

t began with a whisper of motion.

The companions were still in the mayor's study, the empty sword case gleaming mockingly in the firelight, when Kaelen's sharp ears caught the faintest sound – a scuff of leather on stone just beyond the door. His hand went instantly to his bow. "Movement," he hissed.

Before Bramblewood could bark a question, the door cracked open and a shadow slipped inside, darting with impossible speed across the chamber. The intruder's cloak trailed like smoke, their face hidden beneath a hood. They lunged toward the desk, one gloved hand seizing a bundle that glimmered with gemstones.

"The sword!" Bramblewood roared.

Kaelen loosed an arrow in a heartbeat, but the thief twisted like water, the shaft splitting only fabric. The intruder bolted for the hall.

"After them!" Kaelen barked, and the chase began.

The manor erupted with noise – guards shouting, servants screaming – as the companions gave pursuit. The thief moved like quicksilver, weaving through the corridors, vaulting overturned stools and ducking beneath tapestries.

Kaelen sprinted hard, his long strides eating the distance. His ranger's eyes tracked every detail: the smudge of a boot on the carpet, the swing of a door still shuddering from being shoved open. He moved like a hunter, relentless, his quarry in sight.

Tavric was faster in the narrow halls. The halfling darted between startled servants and scattered crockery, his small frame slipping through gaps too tight for the thief. He kept pace with a reckless grin, calling back to the others, "You'd think they'd tidy their corridors for a proper chase!"

Mira ran just behind, her robe tangling around her boots, but her determination outpaced her exhaustion. She raised her holy symbol as she ran, calling out, "By the Morninglord's light – halt!" Her voice rang with authority, and for a heartbeat, the thief faltered, their steps stuttering under the weight of divine command.

It was enough for Serneya. The tiefling's golden eyes blazed as she whispered a phrase that twisted the air. Threads of shimmering energy formed in the corridor, slowing the thief as though they had plunged into a river's current. Their cloak dragged, their limbs heavy.

But the intruder was strong. With a guttural cry, they tore through the spell, crashing shoulder-first into a side door that burst open into the conservatory.

Moonlight poured through the glass ceiling, casting the thief in stark silver and shadow. Orchids trembled as they sprinted past, palms rustled as Kaelen followed close behind.

The ranger nocked another arrow, loosed – this time grazing the thief's shoulder. The figure staggered but pressed on.

Tav darted across a table laden with potted herbs, scattering soil and pots in every direction. He launched himself from the far end, trying to tackle the thief, but his leap only caught the hem of their cloak. He rolled through the fall and bounced to his feet, grinning. "Nearly had you!"

Mira vaulted a low bench, her breath coming hard. She called again, her voice trembling but fierce, "Lathander's light binds you!" The holy symbol flared, casting beams across the glass. The thief threw up an arm against the glare but forced themselves forward.

Serneya strode through the conservatory arch, her cloak rippling though no wind stirred. She raised one hand, her voice low and cutting. "Shadows are not yours to command." The glass lanterns flickered, flames guttering as though recoiling from her. For an instant, the thief slowed – but then they burst through the far doors into the gardens.

The night air hit them like a slap. The gardens sprawled before them, hedges cut in precise lines, gravel paths glittering in the moonlight. The thief darted left, then right, weaving through the maze of greenery.

Kaelen raised his voice. "Cut them off!" He vaulted a hedge, landing lightly in pursuit.

Tav needed no urging. He disappeared into a narrow gap, reappearing two paths over, keeping pace with uncanny precision. "Left! They're going left!" he shouted, his voice carrying through the night.

Mira stumbled briefly on the gravel, but she pushed herself forward, murmuring prayers under her breath. A warm glow flickered at her fingertips, enough to light her way. She kept her eyes fixed on the thief, refusing to fall behind.

Serneya moved with calm determination, her strides unhurried yet inevitable. The shadows themselves seemed to lean toward her, guiding her through the maze.

The thief reached the outer wall, cloak flaring as they scrambled for the trellis. Their muscles coiled, ready to leap –

But Tav burst from the hedge like a spring trap, colliding with the figure at waist height. Both tumbled to the ground in a sprawl of limbs and curses.

Kaelen was on them in a heartbeat, pinning the thief's shoulders, his bowstring taut. Mira grabbed their wrists, holding them fast despite their writhing. Serneya approached last, her golden eyes gleaming as she crouched.

The thief's satchel had spilled open in the fall. From it slid the gem-encrusted ceremonial sword, its hilt glittering like fireflies in the moonlight. Beside it rolled something smaller.

A sphere of black crystal, no larger than a clenched fist, veins of crimson pulsing faintly beneath its surface. It seemed to drink in the moonlight, casting none of its own.

The companions froze. Even Kaelen, his breath hard in his chest, felt the air shift around it. The night grew colder, heavier.

Tav, still straddling the thief, gave a low whistle. "That... is not just stolen goods."

Serneya's gaze locked on the orb. Her voice, when it came, was low, almost reverent. "No. That is something far older."

The Orb pulsed once, faint but unmistakable – like a heartbeat answering theirs.

7

THE SHADOWED RELIC

The gardens of Bramblewood Manor had never known such silence. The usual evening chorus of crickets and nightbirds seemed to hold its breath as the companions crouched around their captive. The thief struggled once more beneath Tavric's knee, but the fight had gone out of them. The gem-encrusted sword gleamed in the grass, but all eyes were fixed on the other object: the black orb.

It lay in the gravel like a drop of solid night, its surface polished to an unnatural sheen. Veins of crimson pulsed faintly beneath the surface, steady as a heartbeat. The moonlight should have revealed its contours, but instead the glow seemed swallowed, devoured, leaving only the faint impression of light fighting to escape.

Kaelen crouched low, his bow still half-drawn. His hand hovered near the orb, but the longer he stared, the stronger his instinct screamed to draw back. "It feels wrong," he said, voice low, as if afraid to wake it. "Like a storm gathering under the skin."

"Don't touch it," Serneya warned, sharper than she intended. The tiefling's golden eyes caught the faint crimson pulse. She could feel the orb pressing against her mind, subtle as a whisper sliding under a locked door. Her fingers twitched against her will, aching to reach for it. "It isn't just an object – it's aware."

The thief gave a bitter laugh, muffled as Mira pressed down harder on his wrists. "You think you're the first to hear it? It whispers. Always whispering. Promises you things, things you didn't know you wanted. And you listen, because... because it already knows you." His voice cracked, and he turned his head away, as if ashamed.

Mira tightened her grip, her expression stern. "Then why steal it? Why endanger others if you knew its nature?"

"I thought I could use it," the thief spat. "Sell it, maybe. Control it. But it doesn't bargain – it *binds*. You carry it too long, and you stop hearing your own thoughts." His eyes darted toward the orb, a flicker of longing betraying his words. "It's like carrying another heartbeat in your chest. At first it's a comfort. Then you realize it isn't yours."

Tav leaned back, keeping his knife ready, his usual smirk dimmed. "So this little bauble's the reason Roric's windmill spins like a drunkard on festival day."

"It's no bauble," Serneya said softly. She rose and circled the orb, each step deliberate, as if afraid the shadows might lash out. "Possession is simple. A ghost grips flesh, a curse gnaws at timber. This is more. It doesn't infect – it reflects. It pushes its will outward, warping what it touches until the world bends to match it."

Kaelen's jaw tightened. "And the windmill was just its toy."

"No," Serneya replied. "Its *signpost*. A warning to those who could see it."

From the far end of the garden came the crunch of hurried boots. Roric emerged, his face pale in the moonlight. He must have followed after them, or perhaps he had been watching all along. His eyes locked on the orb, and the breath left him in a hiss. "I knew it. I *knew* it!"

"You've seen it before?" Kaelen asked.

Roric nodded stiffly. "The night the mill changed, there were shadows at its base. Not natural shadows – these moved like water under a black moon. And in the morning, I found that lying in the grass. I didn't dare touch it. Thought maybe it had vanished. But no... it found new hands."

The orb pulsed once, brighter this time. The crimson veins flared like embers, and the shadows around the hedges seemed to lengthen, stretching toward it. Mira whispered a prayer under her breath, her holy symbol glowing faintly in response.

"It's not safe here," she said. "We can't leave it in the manor."

"Where, then?" Tav asked. "Can't exactly toss it in the river and hope it drowns."

Roric's gaze shifted toward the distant spire of the temple, visible above the rooftops. "Take it to High Priest Aelric. If anyone can cleanse such a thing, it's him. The temple's wards are old, stronger than any lock I could set."

Bramblewood himself appeared then, drawn by the noise. He stopped dead at the sight of the orb, his face draining of color. "By the gods," he whispered. Then, quickly recovering his mayoral bearing, he barked, "Get it out of here. Now. If the villagers even glimpse that, panic will tear Eldermire apart."

Kaelen shouldered his bow, eyeing the orb warily. "Then we'll move fast. Before it finds another way to slip free."

The thief laughed again, hollow and sharp. "You think you carry it? No. It carries you."

Serneya crouched low, her eyes burning. "Enough. You'll speak no more of it." She gestured, and the shadows clamped tighter around the thief's limbs, silencing his protest. But her hands trembled as she drew back.

For even as she commanded the darkness, she could feel the orb whispering still – using her voice, her memories, her long-buried fears. It pressed against her thoughts like a tide against a levee, patient and relentless.

Mira noticed her pallor, but said nothing. She only laid a hand briefly on Serneya's arm, as if to anchor her.

The orb pulsed again, and for a moment every lantern in the manor guttered. Then the light steadied, leaving the companions staring at one another in the uneasy glow.

"Temple," Kaelen said at last. "Before it grows bolder."

Roric nodded, though his eyes never left the orb. "Pray you're not already too late."

8

THE TRIALS

Dawn tinted the temple's marble with a fragile rose. Within Seraphina's nave, High Priest Aelric laid out relics and chalked sigils with a steady hand while the companions listened, shoulders squared not from bravado but from the growing weight of the choice they had already made.

"The Orb of Shadows corrodes through influence rather than impact," Aelric said, voice carrying in the hushed hall. "To cleanse it, you must gather light in three forms: will, mercy, and remembrance." He tapped each diagram on the floor in turn. "A silvered antler from the white stag of Far Tor – symbol of self-governed strength. Tears freely given by the River Lysander's spirit – mercy made manifest. And moonlit moss from Calven's Watch – memory that keeps its glow against darkness."

He looked up. "These are not trophies. They are agreements. Be good to your word, or the ritual will break."

Kaelen nodded once. "We return before moonrise."

Serneya glanced toward the nave's center where the Orb sat in a ring of runes, black as withheld sleep. It pulsed – slow, steady, patient – as if measuring the room's courage in heartbeats. "I'll hold it," she said. "Go."

Kaelen and the White Stag – A Lesson in Will

The hills east of Eldermire rose in softened folds, seam after seam of grass stitched with alder and thorn. Kaelen moved through them the way river-water moves over stone: unhurried, certain. Bristle wheeled above in widening gyres, a dark pen mark written across the morning.

Tracks came first – crescent slots in the drifted damp, clean and deep, weight set evenly. Not a panicked animal. A sovereign. The deer trail threaded between hawthorn clumps heavy with blossom and skirted a chalk outcrop where the wind pooled cool and steady. Kaelen knelt, brushed his fingers along the ground, brought the scent of crushed thyme and clay to his nose. He was not hunting prey; he was approaching a threshold.

By midmorning he found the copse: birch trunks like moonlight hammered into pillars, the understory hushed as if a bell had just been stopped. The white stag stood inside the hush. Its coat was frost at dawn. Its antlers were polished silver, not by craft but by consequence – a sheen like moon trapped in bone. Eyes as dark as seed wells regarded Kaelen, and he felt every lesson he had learned from forests turn inward: breathe with, not against; ask, don't take.

He lowered his bow. He removed his quiver. He unstrung the bow and set it aside. Then he drew a small pouch from his belt – wild thyme, salt, a few grains of barley – and laid them on a flat stone as you might set out words before a friend you haven't yet met.

"I won't chase," Kaelen said, voice even. "We need a tine. Not your life."

The stag's breath misted. It stepped forward once, hooves noiseless in last year's leaves, and tilted its magnificent crown so that one tine kissed the birch. A ring – soft, bell-clear – hung in the air. The tine loosened on its own and fell to the moss with a whisper.

Kaelen exhaled the breath he hadn't realized he held. He picked up the fallen tine, as careful as if cradling a bird. Bristle called from above, satisfied. When Kaelen looked up again, the stag was already mist between the birches, taking the hush with it.

He wrapped the silvered tine in linen. Strength governed is strength offered, he thought, and started back toward the temple.

Mira and the River Spirit – A Testament of Mercy

The River Lysander did not hurry. It braided itself through meadows and under willow canopies, holding sky in its slow curves. Mira followed until she reached a reach where the bank sank gently and pebbles showed bright as coins through the water. The willows there had long fingers and a mother's patience. She knelt, the hem of her robe darkening, and cupped water in her hands. "Lysander," she said softly. "Old friend of root and stone. We ask your tears – freely given – for the cleansing of a harm that was not freely made."

The river listened. Rivers always do, even when their answer is to keep moving.

Mira did not chant her temple's hymns. Instead, she sang a simpler tune, a meadow-plain melody she'd learned from a midwife in a village two countries away. It was a song for cooling fever, for coaxing stubborn infants into breath, for the moment just before dawn when you decide to wait through one more hour. Her voice carried across the water like warm milk poured into a cold cup.

A ripple formed at the center of the bend and came toward her, wider, brighter, lit from beneath by something like moonlight. The spirit rose not as a woman – rivers are not people – but as an agreement shaped like one: shoulders of flowing current, hair of falling water, hands that were onrushing streams made gentle.

"I am not a well to be dipped," the spirit said, voice both rain-on-roof and spring-on-stone.

"I know," Mira replied. "We seek a gift, not a theft."

"What breaks the world asks to be mended by the world," the Lysander murmured, studying her. "How much of you will you spend for a village not yours?"

"As much as it asks," Mira said, and surprised herself with the certainty. Then she added, more quietly, "As little as suffices, so I can keep spending afterward."

The river laughed, the sound sending a shiver through the willow leaves. "Mercy that remembers limits is wiser than sacrifice that forgets. Very well."

The spirit lifted a hand. A single luminous drop formed at her fingertip, heavy as a small truth. When it fell into Mira's cupped palms, it did not vanish; it sat like a pearl, warm, pulsing faintly, a tear that agreed to remain a tear for as long as it needed to be one.

"Guard it," the spirit said. "And when you are asked for mercy you do not think you have, remember me."

"I will," Mira whispered, and the river sank back into itself, the bright growing dim, the world again willow and water and the easy sound of current working out its patient arithmetic.

Mira tucked the tear into a padded vial, sealed it with wax, and turned for home, the melody still sitting at the back of her tongue like a blessing in reserve.

Tav and the Watchtower – A Bargain with Memory

Calven's Watch was less a tower than an intent that had forgotten its body. Stones tumbled from a cliff-edge shelf, blackthorn rooted through the old mortar, and the rope bridge that reached it had learned too much from the wind. Tav stood at the near post, squinting at the sway, weighing risk like a jeweler.

"Right," he told the breeze. "No dying today. I'm booked."

He stepped onto the first plank. It answered with a weary creak. He took another, then another, weighting each, feeling the give, trusting not the rope but his own habit of not falling. Halfway across, a board snapped – clean, efficient – and dropped into the gorge like an idea that had decided to stop pretending.

Tav's legs swung, then his arms were rope, then his breath found the rhythm of pull, brace, reach. He hauled himself up, grinned at no one. "You're going to have to try harder," he informed gravity, and finished the crossing with a lighter step.

Inside the ruin, moonlight fell through a jagged bite in the ceiling though the sun was still up: some places keep their own hours. At the very center where that moonlight always seems to land lay a patch of velveteen moss. It glowed faintly the way old stories do, soaking light and offering it back very slowly.

Tav crouched. "You're gorgeous," he told it. "And I need a bit of you."

He didn't pluck it like a thief snatching a coin. He slid a thin bone spatula beneath an edge, coiled it carefully onto a damp cloth, kept the root-web intact – memory is in the roots, after all. As he worked, a draft crossed the ruin, cold as a cellar thought. The Orb's whisper arrived a heartbeat later, wearing his voice as a mask.

You're clever. You're quick. Imagine what you could do if doors never shut to you again.

Tav's hands paused. "Tempting," he admitted – to the air, to himself. He pictured vaults that bloomed open, secrets that lifted their hems. He pictured the look on certain faces he'd met in certain cities. Then he pictured the mill's stubborn sails, children's eyes following their spin with a fear they wouldn't name.

"Nah," he said aloud. "I already like who I am when doors are hard." He bundled the moss gently, slid it into a tin lined with damp paper, and eased back across the bridge – step, test, step – whistling a tune about a sailor who forgot which way was forward and ended up exactly where he meant.

Serneya's Vigil – A Wall Against the Tide

While the others navigated hill and river and ruin, Serneya remained within the temple's drawn circle. The Orb sat in the sigils like a night bruise. It did not rage. It suggested. It offered.

We are the same, it said in the voice of a girl she had once been – the one who had counted the knots in a tenement ceiling and found constellations there. *Outsiders. Misunderstood. We could make a covenant, you and I. You would never be alone in your mind again.*

Serneya had been alone in rooms crowded with people and at home in rooms with no one in them. Loneliness no longer frightened her; the wrong kind of company did. She breathed through the whispers and fed the circle with quiet power, small renewals – like stoking embers rather than calling lightning.

At noon, she pressed her palm to the outer line and felt it hungry for steadiness. She hummed low, a note her patron had taught her – a chord that made shadow remember it came after light, not before.

At midafternoon, the Orb found a seam in her guard. It slipped through on a remembered scent: cinnamon pastry, hot from an oven on a street two cities away. Her throat tightened; her mouth watered. The memory widened. For a moment her fingers twitched toward the Orb, not with fear but with nostalgia.

She laughed – soft, surprised – and the nostalgia thinned. "Oh, you are good," she said. "You're not getting better."

She chalked another ring. Wards don't have to be beautiful to work, but these were. She permitted herself that. Beauty is a kind of refusal.

As shadows lengthened, the Orb pulsed faster, tasting the air for companions returning. Serneya set her hand to the marble and whispered, "Hold," to both the circle and herself.

Return – Three Gifts, One Chance

They came back in staggered light: Kaelen first, a silvered tine wrapped in linen, the smell of birch still in his cloak. Mira next, a vial in her palm with a single luminous tear suspended as if the world had agreed, just this once, to pause gravity. Tav last, whistling, tin under his arm, a smear of chalk on his cheek from a kiss with an old wall.

Aelric met them at the nave's threshold with relief carefully folded into ritual dignity. "Set them there," he said, indicating three petaled circles radiating from the Orb's ring. "Do not cross the lines."

Kaelen placed the antler like one warrior yielding to another. Mira set the vial down as if laying a sleeping child to rest. Tav eased the tin open and unrolled the moss, the faint glow quickening like someone waking without alarm.

The temple exhaled. Even the sconces seemed to nod. Serneya felt the pressure shift – the way heavy weather sometimes lifts a fraction before the storm arrives.

"Will," Aelric intoned, touching the antler. "Mercy," he said, and his fingers warmed the glass. "Remembrance," and he brushed the moss like a page.

He looked up at the companions. "You've brought the agreements. Now we must keep them. When we begin, you will be tempted not by what you fear but by what you almost want. If you doubt, look to one another."

The Orb answered with a pulse that rattled the lantern glass, not a threat, not even a boast – acknowledgment. It had been met in kind.

Serneya's eyes found each of her friends in turn – Kaelen with river-weather in his hair, Mira with willow-light in her gaze, Tav smelling faintly of moon and chalk – and felt the small, private warmth of being part of an exact number.

"Then let's finish what we started," she said.

Outside, evening began to gather its blue. Inside, gold dust waited for the first spark.

9

BETWEEN LIGHT AND SHADOW

The sun was sinking when the companions returned to Seraphina's Temple, its last gold painting the marble steps in honeyed light. From three different paths they came – Kaelen from the hills, Mira from the river, Tavric from the broken watchtower – and though their strides were weary, there was a quiet resolve in each.

High Priest Aelric stood waiting at the temple doors, the Orb's faint pulse already pressing against the wards within. His lined face betrayed little, but the faint sag of his shoulders told of a long day spent shoring up protections that barely held. "You have them?" he asked, his voice carrying across the nave.

Kaelen stepped forward first, holding out the wrapped silver tine. He unrolled the linen with reverence, revealing the antler's sheen – moonlight trapped in bone. "The stag gave freely," he said. "A gift, not a trophy."

Mira followed, her hands cradling the small vial sealed with wax. Inside shimmered the tear, glowing faintly as if it still remembered the river's current. "The Lysander spirit wept willingly. But she warned me: mercy that spends too much may burn itself away."

Tav came last, setting his tin carefully on the altar steps. He popped it open and peeled back the damp cloth to reveal the moss, its faint glow steady and stubborn. "Moonlit moss from Calven's Watch," he said, dusting his hands. "Bridge nearly killed me. But memory held." His grin was quick, but his eyes were shadowed.

Aelric inclined his head. "Three lights gathered. Three agreements kept. It will be enough – if your hearts hold."

The Orb pulsed in its circle at the nave's center, as though mocking the declaration. The crimson veins flickered faster, like laughter beating inside the crystal.

Serneya had not moved since dawn. She still knelt within the wards, her hands pressed to the sigils etched in gold dust. Her face was pale, and her lips bore the faint cracks of whispered incantations repeated without pause. But her eyes, golden and unblinking, lifted now to meet theirs.

"You're late," she murmured, voice hoarse. "It's been talking all day."

Mira knelt beside her at once, setting a hand on her shoulder. "And you resisted?"

Serneya gave a humorless smile. "I've had practice ignoring voices that pretend they know me." She leaned closer, her tone soft enough only the party could hear. "But it's clever. It found pieces of me I'd rather forget. I won't last another night."

Kaelen glanced at the High Priest. "Then we act before moonrise."

They gathered in the side chamber where offerings were prepared. It was quiet there, the marble cool beneath their boots, the air scented faintly with incense burned earlier in the day. Candles flickered, casting light that wavered like thought itself.

It was Tav, of all of them, who broke the silence first. He tossed a small pebble he'd pocketed during his bridge crossing from hand to hand. "So. We're about to sit in a circle and tell an ancient evil it's not welcome. Anybody want to admit they're terrified?"

Kaelen gave him a flat look, but Mira surprised them all by answering, "I am." She lifted her chin, unashamed. "The Orb is older than any of us, older than Eldermire, maybe older than kingdoms. Fear is the right response. But so is courage."

Her words settled like warm bread shared on a cold morning.

Kaelen leaned against the wall, arms crossed. "Fear keeps the hand steady. Too much, and it shakes. I'll find the balance." His voice carried the certainty of someone who had hunted enough nights to know the measure of his own nerves.

Tav grinned faintly. "That's ranger talk for 'yes, but I'll never admit it.' Noted."

Serneya sat apart, her back to the cold stone. She turned her hands over, studying the faint tremble in her fingers. "I won't lie. The Orb and I... spoke. It wanted me to believe we were kin. It nearly succeeded." Her golden eyes lifted, hardening. "If I falter, you must not hesitate. Even if it's me you need to restrain."

Mira reached across the space and covered her hand. "Then none of us falters. Not tonight."

For a moment, there was nothing but the sound of their breaths and the faint groan of the windmill's sails outside, still fighting the breeze as though reminding them of the stakes.

Aelric entered then, carrying a bowl of sanctified oil and a brazier of burning herbs. His expression was solemn. "The circle is ready. Once we begin, you cannot step back. Each of you will be tested – not by what you fear most, but by what you *almost* desire. That is how shadow snares."

He set the bowl on the altar and looked at each in turn. "If you doubt, look to one another. Alone, you will break. Together, you may endure."

The companions exchanged glances. Kaelen's eyes were steady, Mira's shone with quiet fire, Tav's grin returned – thinner now, but no less stubborn – and Serneya's gaze burned with a resolve sharpened by defiance.

They rose, each bearing the weight of what they had gathered: silvered will, merciful tear, steadfast memory. The nave awaited, the Orb pulsing like a heart already beating for their failure.

Kaelen drew in a long breath. "Then let's not keep it waiting."

And together, they stepped back into the temple, into the circle, into the waiting shadow.

10

THE CLEANSING

The nave of Seraphina's Temple had been remade into a compass of light.

Gold dust traced a wide circle on the marble floor, its edge as precise as a knife's rim. Three smaller petals unfurled from the circumference toward the center, and in each rested a gathered light: Kaelen's silvered tine wrapped and unwrapped until it shone like a captured crescent; Mira's vial, a single luminous tear refusing to fall; Tav's pillow of moonlit moss, still faintly aglow as if remembering an older sky. At the center of it all, nested inside a ring of interlocking sigils, the Orb of Shadows pulsed with patient malice – black glass threaded with embers – like a coal that had outlived the fire that birthed it.

High Priest Aelric moved with the deliberate grace of a man who had performed countless rites and never once mistaken habit for certainty. He set a brazier at the north point of the circle and a shallow bowl of sanctified oil at the south. Incense breathed a clean, resinous scent. Torches guttered as if taking shorter breaths.

"Once begun, we do not break the circle," Aelric said. "If anyone steps through, the light will tear – and the shadow will tear with it." He looked at each of them in turn. "Be as you promised: will, mercy, remembrance."

Kaelen set the antler on its petal and straightened. The ranger's hands were steady; his eyes were not. They tracked the Orb with an animal's mistrust of what does not act like the world. Mira set the vial down as a midwife might lay a sleeping child, her lips moving through a private prayer. Tav unrolled the moss, smoothing its edges with surprising tenderness, as if coaxing a skittish cat into a sunbeam. Serneya knelt at the circle's rim, fingers already finding the first syllables of the containment hymn, her golden eyes narrowed not with fear but with refusal.

Aelric joined her in the hymn, then shifted to a ringing cantillation that filled the high, vaulted space. The words were old – older than the temple – chosen more for their shape in the mouth than for any meaning anyone now remembered. Sound became scaffold. Breath became scaffold. Together they built a frame strong enough to hold a darkness that could not bear containment.

The Orb answered immediately.

It did not leap or start; it widened. The black beneath its surface deepened, swallowing the light that fell upon it. The crimson veins brightened and pulsed so slowly that for a moment the eye thought the beating belonged to the watcher. The first tendrils of shadow rose like steam off a winter road, soft and almost pretty, and then thickened into cords that lashed at the edge of the sigils. Kaelen's bow was in his hand without memory of drawing it. He loosed an arrow into the nearest tendril; the shaft hissed as if passing through sleet and tore the shadow apart into a fine, glittering haze that smelled faintly of iron. The haze drifted back toward the Orb like smoke committing to its chimney.

Mira lifted her holy symbol. Light gathered at its center, not a flash but a swelling – warm, steady, like a lantern fed with fresh oil. She raised it high. "By morning's mercies," she said, and the words struck the nearest cords like hot wire through frost. They shrank away, but not before one licked at her forearm. Cold burned there, a line that felt like absence and left gooseflesh in its wake.

Tav stayed low and close to the ring, knife out, watching where the tendrils sought thinness in the dust lines. Each time one crept toward a crack, he slashed – not to cut shadow (the blade went through like water) but to kick a spill of fresh gold dust across the gap, resealing the drawn geometry. "Circles," he muttered, almost cheerfully in the way of a man who refused to surrender humor to dread, "are just polite ways of saying no."

Serneya's voice layered under Aelric's, then around it, a lower register that made the gold dust shiver. To the Orb she spoke without words: *You will find no agreement here.* The Orb replied in voices that were almost hers. *We are kin. No one else knows you as I do.* The cadence of her chant did not falter, but a vein stood out at her throat.

Aelric reached into the bowl, anointed the antler with sanctified oil, and tilted it toward the Orb. "Will," he intoned. The silvered tine drank the light along its length and threw it into the circle as a crescent arc. The tendrils that touched that crescent recoiled as if struck by their own memory of choice – whatever the Orb had bound inside it, the act of binding did not erase the knowledge of freedom. The antler brightened, then steadied, settling into a constant, quiet glow.

The Orb tested another seam in the circle. The torches along the nave dimmed; shadows thickened by the pillars; the brazier hissed and dropped a cinder like a red star falling. The temperature fell not with a sudden rush but with an inexorable thinning, the way a fever breaks into the wrong kind of chill.

Aelric uncorked the vial in Mira's hands. As the stopper left the glass, the tear inside swelled – not to fall but to be the shape of falling forever. He let a single drop of that light tip into the ring. Where it touched the marble, the stone brightened – not merely painted brighter, but *made* brighter, as if the floor remembered a brief, unblemished morning from its quarry's youth. "Mercy," he said, and the word went out across the ring like water finding low ground.

The Orb's answer was cunning. Not a lash. An invitation.

Kaelen heard leaves in high wind, the soft heavy footfall of a stag, and then – someone saying his name in a voice he had not permitted himself to imagine in years. The air before him thickened, then clarified into the shape of a young man with a crooked smile and river-mud on his boots. "You left," the apparition said, not accusingly but with that simple bewilderment the dead have for the living's departures. "You could stop leaving. Stay. I'll stay."

Kaelen's hand shook. The arrow's fletching rasped his cheek. He had the absurd thought that if he loosed now, the shaft would pass through and he would finally know the answer to a question he did not allow himself to name. Somewhere far away he heard Tav's knife scrape stone; Serneya's voice tightened; Mira's breath catch. He lowered the bow.

Then he forced himself to look *down*, not ahead – at the circle. At the crisp gold line he had promised not to cross. He breathed in through his nose, out through his mouth, the way he had taught himself to breathe on nights when solitude pressed its knee to his chest.

"I leave because I go," he said, voice steadying. "Because going is the work." He raised the bow again – not to fire through the image, but to aim past it, at the Orb. "You're not him."

The apparition flickered. The Orb's pulse stuttered once, then resumed.

Mira's temptation came like a door flung open into a room she had always wanted to enter. In it, no child ever died half a day after fever broke; no mother bled out quietly because the midwife arrived half a breath late; no soldier came home without pieces of himself useful to joy. She could feel the heat of hundreds of foreheads under her palm – cooling, cooling, cooling. The Orb offered her capacity multiplied past reason. *Give me your limits,* it whispered in the kindly voice of an elder sister she had never had, *and I will give you ends to grief you have earned the right to end.*

Her knees trembled. Behind the offer, though, she smelled the slick of burnt oil when a lamp is turned too high and then quietly dies. Mercy that burned itself to ash could pour nothing tomorrow. She pressed her thumb hard into the base of her holy symbol until pain clarified into boundary. "I am finite," she said, and the words felt like profanity and promise at once. "That is how mercy survives."

The light at the symbol's heart steadied – smaller than she wanted, but truer.

Tav's test arrived wearing velvet and laughter. Vaults despaired of him. Hinges failed rather than insult him with resistance. Every lock offered its throat like a puppy. Every closed room in every high house, every sealed ledger in every cruel hand, every secret that made small people small – opened. He could hear the clean click of tumblers surrendering as a kind of music. He almost laughed at the sheer rightness of it. *You'd do good,* the Orb cooed, not lying – merely rearranging truth. *You'd do it faster.*

Tav breathed out a single word through his teeth. "Boring." He said it lightly, but a tenderness came with it – toward the parts of himself that liked difficulty because overcoming it had taught him who he was. He slashed a neat line of gold across a tiny crack the shadow had been fingering, and the seam sealed with a bright sneeze of light. "I like doors that say maybe."

Serneya's turn did not arrive; it had never left. The Orb knew where to push. It wore her childhood's soot – counted her tenement's thin winter windows back to her and offered her a room warmed with a fire that answered to her thought. It found the older bad nights too, the ones with the wrong company – men who smiled with every tooth and said *we* when they meant *you, but inside my future.* It offered her a pronoun that would never again leave her stranded: *ours.*

She let the loneliness pass through her like a weather front and did not argue its sky. She did not pretend she hadn't wanted the thing offered. She did not slap her own hand. She named the wanting, and the naming made a door. Wanting behind a door is not a master. "You call it covenant," she told the Orb, voice flat. "You mean custody."

Her chant changed key. The ring brightened as if someone had rolled a richer sun from the sacristy and set it just out of sight. The Orb's veins fluttered, then beat harder.

Aelric tipped the vial and traced a wet circle inside the gold. The tear did not spread like water; it kept its droplet integrity at every point it touched, as if hundreds of tiny tears agreed to become a ring together. The temperature rose a breath. The air tasted briefly of willow tea. "Mercy binds," he said, and this time it was not instruction but memory.

"Remembrance holds," Serneya added, nodding to Tav. He lifted the moss and blew across it gently. The glow brightened, not to dazzle but to persist – the light of coals in a hearth at midnight, promising morning.

"Will chooses," Kaelen finished, and placed the antler's tip precisely where the three petal-lines met.

The circle tightened. The Orb shook. The first true scream came – soundless, but the kind that makes eardrums feel licked by knives. The crimson veins flared, then split like struck lacquer. Shadow spilled, furious now, no more tendrils or cunning apparitions – just the raw, thrashing insistence of a thing that had forgotten any language but possession.

The circle held. Barely.

Cracks chased each other along the black surface, spiderwebbing outward from a hairline fracture near the Orb's heart. It tried one last thing – the basest and oldest: brute cold. Frost flowered across the marble in branching ferns that sought ankles and wrists. Mira's breath smoked; Kaelen's bowstring creaked as ice kissed it; Tav's blade stuck to his palm and he peeled it free with a curse. Serneya's lips went white.

"Now," Aelric said, voice not raised but deepened. "Together."

Kaelen lowered his bow and set his hands on the ring, not crossing it. "Here."

Mira set her palm beside his. "Here."

Tav flattened his hand on the cold marble, grin gone, eyes bright. "Here."

Serneya laid her hands last and closed her eyes. "Here."

The circle answered *there*, which is the only word circles have. The gold flared, the tear brightened without losing itself, the moss held steady like a lighthouse whispering instead of shouting. Under their hands the marble warmed. Above their heads the temple's vaulted ceiling swallowed the scream Whole. The Orb's veins flickered in panic, then snuffed in patches. The cracks deepened.

"Hold," Aelric said, and they did – not with force, but with refusal that had remembered its reasons.

The Orb imploded not with a bang but with a soft, appalling relief – as when a boil is lanced, as when a lie finally collapses under the weight of itself. Black glass crushed inward, then sifted outward into ash so fine it looked like a shadow exhaling. The cold dropped away. The torches steadied. The ring of tiny tears evaporated with the faintest chime, like ice melting in a glass across a warm room. Silence blew through the nave. Long, clean, and fragile.

Aelric sagged back on his heels, then bowed his head. "It is done," he said, not as a priest pronouncing but as a man admitting.

Kaelen released a breath that shook more than he liked and let his hands fall to his thighs. Mira's palms were red where she had pressed the marble; she flexed them and laughed once – wet, surprised. Tav fell backward, sprawled, stared at the ceiling beams, and said, "I am very interested in an un-cursed pastry." Serneya opened her eyes last.

For a heartbeat, she thought she saw the ash stir – not to gather, not to return, but the way dust lifts when someone passes down a hall two rooms away. A memory of movement rather than movement. She tucked the noticing into the careful place where she kept things that were true but not urgent.

Aelric rose, slower than he had knelt, and made a sign over the circle. "What was bound here will not trouble Eldermire again," he said. "What begot it – well. Shadows do not spring from nothing."

Mira corked the empty vial and slipped it back into her pouch. "Then we have bought morning," she said, "and some days beyond."

Kaelen brushed a smear of gray from the antler and wrapped it once more. "Morning's enough to start," he said.

Tav pinched a fleck of ash between finger and thumb, held it up to the light, then let it go. It drifted and vanished in sunbeams laid across the nave. "And if the afternoon tries something foolish," he added, the grin returning slow as dawn, "we'll be rude about it."

Serneya rose, bones creaking as if she had stood watch through a winter. "Let's tell Roric," she said, and her voice held something like warmth. "The wind ought to remember which way to turn."

11

RETURN TO ELDERMIRE

Morning broke with the clarity of glass. The storm that had not been weather had lifted, leaving the sky polished, the air as fresh as springwater. The companions stepped out of the temple's high doors into light that felt sharper than the day before, as if the world itself had been scoured clean. Birds sang from the eaves, and somewhere a rooster crowed, absurdly late, as though it too had waited for the night to end.

The road back to Eldermire wound through orchards alive with bees and hedges wet with dew. The companions rode in silence at first. Their bodies were weary, bruised in spirit if not in flesh, yet there was a lightness under their fatigue – a taut rope cut free, a burden eased.

Kaelen rode at the front, Bristle circling overhead. The hawk's wings caught the morning sun, bright flashes like silver coins cast into the air. Kaelen's gaze stayed on the horizon, but his ears twitched every time the breeze shifted. He was listening not just for danger but for what had changed, cataloguing how the air no longer carried that unnatural pressure.

Mira rode close behind, her face lifted toward the light. She whispered a prayer not of request but of thanks, words simple as bread. Her hand brushed the sunburst pendant at her chest, and for once she felt it hum faintly in reply. The Orb's temptation had left her shaken, but the morning air tasted of promise – fragile, yes, but true.

Tav had abandoned silence entirely. He sat sideways in his saddle, hands behind his head, whistling a jaunty tune that skittered up and down the scale with no regard for rhythm. "You know," he said cheerfully, "there's nothing like almost dying in a temple to make you appreciate breakfast. I hope someone's already turning out pies. Cider. Both. At once."

Serneya trailed slightly behind, her hood low. Her golden eyes did not seek the sun. They lingered on the road itself, on the shadows beneath the hedges, on the way ash sometimes lifted in the breeze only to vanish before she could be sure she had seen it. She said nothing. The others did not press her.

By the time the village came into view, the air was buzzing with a quiet energy. Eldermire looked the same – cobbled lanes, ivy-draped cottages, children chasing one another across the green

– but the posture of the people had shifted. Men straightened from their plows with surprise, as though a weight had slid from their shoulders overnight. Women at the well whispered, glancing toward the hill. Children pointed, eyes wide.

The windmill turned.

Its sails, once stubborn, now moved in steady harmony with the morning breeze. No grinding, no groaning – only the smooth, rhythmic creak of timber doing the work it was meant to do. Even at a distance, the change was undeniable.

At its base stood Roric. His broad frame was set against the stone, one hand splayed across it as though to feel the pulse of the machine. He lifted his head as the companions rode near. The suspicion that had first greeted them was gone. In its place was something rawer, harder for him to show: relief.

"You did it," he called, his voice carrying across the field. "It must've been the Orb!"

Kaelen dismounted first, the crunch of boots on gravel deliberate, steady. "The windmill's yours again," he said. "It'll listen to the wind now, not to shadows."

Roric's hand lingered on the wall. His pale eyes shifted from Kaelen to Mira, to Tav, to Serneya. "I've kept this mill running twenty years," he said slowly. "I thought I knew every complaint of its gears, every shiver of its sails. But this…" He shook his head. "This was older than me. Older than the village. I'd have been lost without you."

Mira smiled gently. "You were never meant to carry it alone."

Roric exhaled, a sound caught between a sigh and a laugh. "Well, alone's what I'm best at. But maybe not forever." He straightened, brushing flour dust from his tunic. "Come back tonight, if you'll stay. Eldermire will want to thank you. And I owe you cider."

Tav perked at the word. "Finally. The man speaks my language."

But Kaelen shook his head. "We'll ride on before dusk." His voice was calm, but firm. Hunters never linger too long in the clearing once the quarry's down.

The village gathered as they turned their mounts. Children waved, a few bold ones calling thanks. Farmers dipped their heads. A baker pressed a loaf into Mira's hands, warm from the oven. No one spoke of the Orb. They didn't need to. They only knew that the wind had remembered its way.

At the edge of the green, Mira glanced back. Roric still stood by the mill, one hand raised in farewell. The sails turned smooth above him, steady as a heartbeat.

Kaelen followed her gaze, then looked away first. Tav winked at a cluster of giggling children and tipped his patched cap. Serneya lingered longest, her eyes fixed on the sails. For just a heartbeat, she thought she saw the faintest shimmer near the mill's base – a curl of ash catching the breeze, twisting upward into a shape almost human before it scattered.

She said nothing.

The companions left Eldermire with the wind at their backs. The fields stretched wide, the road long, the morning bright. The village had been delivered its morning; the companions carried forward something else entirely – knowledge that shadows did not vanish, only waited.

12

RESURRECTION

They left Eldermire beneath a sky rinsed clean by dawn. The road stretched before them, damp with dew, its edges bordered by hedgerows alive with sparrows and foxgloves. Behind them, the village began to stir into ordinary life: smoke rising from chimneys, sheep driven to pasture, bakers kneading dough with flour-dusted hands. For the first time in weeks, Eldermire woke without dread.

Yet for the companions, leaving was never simply leaving. They carried more than saddle bags and coin pouches. They carried the weight of what they had seen and what they had withstood – the whispers of a shadow that had nearly found a voice in each of them.

Kaelen rode at the front, Bristle circling high above in wide arcs, as if scouting not for prey but for horizons. The half-elf's expression was unreadable, but his eyes never left the shifting line where sky met land. He had stared into the shape of someone he had lost and chosen to walk away. That choice still burned in his chest, an ache that was both wound and healing. His hand brushed the silvered antler tied at his saddle. The stag's gift was a reminder: strength was not in never leaving, but in carrying forward.

Mira rode beside him, sunlight catching the edge of her pendant. She had knelt before the mercy of the River Lysander and been tempted to become endless. Yet she had chosen her limits, and now those limits felt like armor rather than chains. She glanced at the children playing in Eldermire's fields as they passed – their laughter rising clean and unburdened – and thought of the tear sealed once in her vial. It was gone, consumed in the ritual, but the lesson of it lingered: that mercy's strength lay not in infinite supply but in knowing when to pour and when to rest.

Behind them, Tav whistled a half-forgotten tune, jaunty as ever, but his eyes flicked often to the roadside hedges, the stone fences, the locks on farmhouse doors. The Orb had whispered that every barrier could be his to open, every secret his to claim. He had turned it aside with a joke, but the echo lingered. There was a strange comfort in difficulty, he realized, in locks that resisted, in doors that said "maybe." Without resistance, he was not himself.

He tapped the tin that once held the moss against his thigh and grinned to no one in particular. "Still like doors," he muttered.

Serneya brought up the rear, her cloak brushing the dust of the road. The others left behind temptation; she carried temptation still. The Orb had courted her loneliness with promises of belonging, its voice soft as a lullaby. She had denied it, but the denial did not erase the wanting. She had heard it call her kin, and part of her – small, secret, unspoken – had not entirely disagreed. Her golden eyes lingered on every shadow the morning cast, searching for movement that wasn't there. When she looked back at Eldermire one last time, she thought she saw ash rise in the distance, a brief coil twisting into a shape almost human before the wind carried it away. She said nothing.

The road carried them to a crossroads as the sun climbed. Three paths split before them: north into mountains lined with silver pines, west toward the coast where the air smelled faintly of salt, and east into a forest dark with tangled green.

Kaelen slowed his horse, the others drawing alongside. "We've a choice," he said simply.

"West," Tav said immediately, patting his stomach. "There's a port town that brews cider strong enough to make you forget your own name."

"East," Mira countered gently. "Villages in the deepwood struggle this time of year. I've heard rumors of sickness spreading where wells run shallow."

Kaelen glanced at Serneya. She said nothing, but her gaze had already settled on the forest road. The shadows beneath the trees looked deeper than they should, darker than noon ought to allow.

Kaelen gave a short nod. "East, then."

Tav groaned but didn't argue. "Fine. But if we save another cursed village, you all owe me pie."

They nudged their mounts forward. The dust lifted at their passing, drifting briefly in the air before settling again. Villagers working their fields paused to watch the four figures ride toward the trees, whispers following them like soft prayers.

At the crest of the rise, the party looked back one last time. Eldermire lay small in the valley now, its windmill sails turning obediently with the breeze. Roric stood near its base, his hand lifted in farewell. The sight should have been enough to close the book.

But stories never close so neatly.

The companions turned east, their silhouettes thinning into the line of the forest. The road ahead was unknown, but the road behind had taught them this: that the world spun not just on wind and stone, but on choices – on mercy given, on strength tempered, on limits honored, on belonging chosen.

And somewhere beyond the horizon, shadows waited for their next turn at the wheel.

E

EPILOGUE

Night had returned to Eldermire, soft and ordinary. Lanterns glowed in windows, smoke curled lazily from chimneys, and the fields slept under the hush of spring. To anyone walking the cobblestone lanes, the village seemed mended, its days no longer ruled by unease.

And yet, not all wounds vanish so swiftly.

Roric stood at the foot of the windmill, hand pressed to its stone foundation. The sails turned with the wind now, steady and true, but each creak made him flinch. He had taken to sleeping in fits, rising at odd hours to check the gears, to assure himself it was still only wood and stone at work. Sometimes, in the silence before dawn, he swore he heard the faint hum below. Not loud. Not threatening. Just there. A memory, or a reminder.

He closed his eyes and whispered a prayer – not to Seraphina, not even to Lathander, but to the nameless keeping of ordinary things. Let the mill stay what it is. Let the sails obey the breeze.

The village, though, did not forget easily. Children dared one another to run up the hill at night and touch the mill's base. Farmers crossed themselves when they walked past. Mothers hushed the talk, but whispers ran through the inn like an undercurrent: the windmill had been wrong, and strangers had set it right. For now.

In the temple, High Priest Aelric lingered by the nave long after the last worshippers had gone. The cleansing circle had been swept, the gold dust collected, but faint gray ash still clung in the cracks of the marble. He traced it with one finger, thoughtful.

The Orb was gone, reduced to fragments finer than breath. But Aelric knew enough of relics and curses to understand that destruction was seldom absolute. Shadows scattered, yes – but shadows always gathered again. Not here, perhaps. Not tomorrow. But somewhere.

"Mercy binds," he murmured, recalling the words he had spoken during the ritual. He let his hand fall, heavy with doubt. "But mercy alone does not end a war."

Far down the eastern road, beyond the orchards and hedgerows, four travelers made camp at the edge of the forest. Their fire burned low, throwing sparks into the dark canopy above.

Kaelen sat a little apart, whittling a fallen branch into a shaft, his knife sure and quiet. Bristle perched nearby, feathers ruffling as she preened. The ranger's gaze was on the flames, but his ears twitched at every sound from the trees. He had chosen east because the shadows in the forest had felt wrong, but he hadn't told the others the full truth: he had seen something move in them when they left Eldermire. Small, quick, watching.

Mira tended the fire, feeding it with careful patience. She hummed under her breath, a tune from her temple, and though it was soft, it steadied the night. The Orb had tempted her with boundless mercy, but tonight she found strength in small acts – one log at a time, one prayer at a time, one warmth at a time.

Tav lay flat on his back, staring at the stars. "If cursed windmills are what farming folk build over their cellars, I can't wait to see what lunacy cities hide." His grin flickered in the firelight, but there was something harder beneath it. He had heard his own voice in the Orb's promises, and no jest could erase that entirely. Still, he would whistle tomorrow, and the next, because whistling kept the silence from creeping in.

Serneya sat closest to the trees, golden eyes reflecting both flame and shadow. Her hands rested still on her knees, but her mind was far from the camp. She could still hear it – the whisper the Orb had spoken in her own voice, calling her kin. Even shattered, even ash, its echo lingered. She feared that what had been bound in Eldermire was only a fragment, one of many seeds scattered through the world.

When she glanced toward the fire, she found Mira watching her. The cleric smiled gently, no question in her eyes, only trust. Serneya inclined her head, the faintest acknowledgment, then turned back to the forest.

The night deepened. The forest sighed. Somewhere an owl called, and the horses shifted uneasily. The companions did not speak again before sleep.

Far from Eldermire, across plains and rivers, beyond mountains where snow lingered eternal, a cavern lay forgotten. Its walls glistened with veins of stone like frozen lightning. At its center stood a pedestal much like the one beneath the mill, carved of the same granite, waiting in silence.

On it rested an orb.

Black. Veined with crimson.

It pulsed once.

And the shadows around it stirred.

C

MEET THE COMPANIONS

Before the story begins, it is worth knowing the four who ride together into Eldermire. Each comes from a different corner of the world, carrying their own burdens, strengths, and secrets. They are bound not by shared homeland or blood, but by the kind of fellowship that grows only in danger and on the road.

Kaelen Thorne – Half-elf Ranger

Kaelen was born in the Ashwood borderlands, where shifting alliances and harsh winters taught him early to survive by instinct rather than trust. His father, an elf of the deep woods, gave him patience and a hunter's eye; his mother, a human trader, gave him adaptability and a wary respect for people's duplicity. Kaelen has never cared for politics or polished words – he believes truth lies in tracks on the ground, in the lean of branches, in the silence of a forest before a storm.

He is sharp-eyed and quiet, a man who speaks sparingly but whose words cut to the point when he does. His closest bond is not to any town or family but to Bristle, his hawk companion. Bristle's keen sight often sees what Kaelen cannot, and the ranger trusts the bird as he trusts his own bow. Together they move with an efficiency that others mistake for aloofness – but those who have stood beside Kaelen in battle know his loyalty is as steadfast as oak.

Mira Valeheart – Human Cleric of Lathander

Mira was raised in a temple of Lathander, where she learned that hope is not a prayer whispered in safety, but a light carried into darkness. She is bright-eyed, with a warmth that disarms suspicion, and she walks into every town as if it were her duty to heal not only bodies but spirits. Injustices pull at her like magnets; suffering draws her with the same inevitability as sunrise.

Her healing magic is rooted in stubborn faith, but Mira's real strength lies in her unwillingness to look away. She asks questions others prefer to leave unspoken – of leaders, of priests, of her companions, and even of herself. She believes mercy is strength, though she has yet to fully reconcile the limits of her own humanity with her desire to mend all wounds.

To her companions, Mira is often the conscience and the center: a voice reminding them why they fight, a hand steady on a shoulder when shadows press too close.

Tavric "Tav" Underbough – Halfling Rogue

If Kaelen is the hunter and Mira the healer, Tavric is the trouble you never saw coming until it was already grinning in your face. Born in a bustling trade town, Tav learned quickly that nimble fingers and a quicker wit could get him further than honest labor. He insists, loudly and often, that he is now "reformed" – though his friends know the truth: temptation follows him like his own shadow, and he rarely tries very hard to outrun it.

Tav is quick-witted, silver-tongued, and has an unshakable talent for finding the one locked chest, hidden door, or unguarded pie that others overlook. He masks fear with humor and shame with swagger, but beneath the mischief lies loyalty he would never admit aloud. To his companions, Tav is equal parts exasperation and necessity – he can charm information from a wary innkeeper, slip through a bolted window, or turn disaster into opportunity with a smile that borders on reckless.

If the group is a blade, Tav is its edge: unpredictable, sharp, and occasionally dangerous even to the hand that holds it.

Serenya Duskbane – Tiefling Warlock

Serenya carries her heritage like a shadow: horns that curve black as midnight, skin the shade of dusk, and eyes molten gold that see both more and less than the world offers. Many call her cursed, yet she claims her power from a pact not with demon or devil but with a celestial being – mysterious, distant, and more cryptic than comforting. The bond grants her strange magic and visions that arrive like riddles: sometimes a warning, sometimes a curse, always too much or too little, never precisely when she wishes.

She speaks less than Tav, laughs less than Mira, and trusts less than Kaelen. Yet when her voice does rise, her companions listen, for it often carries truths too sharp to ignore. She is haunted not only by the whispers of her patron but by her own hunger for belonging, a hunger the Orb of Shadows will one day exploit.

To the world, Serneya is an enigma. To her companions, she is a question with no easy answer – one they have chosen, again and again, to keep at their side.

Together, these four ride toward Eldermire: a ranger with a hawk's eyes, a cleric with a sunlit heart, a rogue with a shadow's grin, and a warlock with a darkness she will not name. Whatever waits in the turning sails of the windmill, they will face it as they face all things: uneasily, imperfectly, and together.

About the Author

JPS Nagi resides in the picturesque Pacific Northwest, where towering evergreens and misty mornings shape both his days and his imagination. He shares life's adventures with his wife, two children, and their spirited Maltese dog, Snowy – named after Tintin's faithful companion.

JPS finds joy in exploring new ideas, playing board games, and, more recently, diving deep into the boundless worlds of role-playing games. These passions fuel his storytelling, inspiring tales where chance, choice, and imagination converge.

When not writing fantasy adventures, he curates his personal blog, Planet Nagi, a constellation of musings (Soliloquy) and original stories (Inked Orbits) that reflect his love for words and the many worlds they create.

www.PlanetNagi.com

www.ingramcontent.com/pod-product-compliance
Lightning Source LLC
Chambersburg PA
CBHW052014170626
46808CB00007B/2929